Ricky Dale's

Double Entendre

To my grandson Oakley Jay

Published by Ricky Dale

Publishing partner: Paragon Publishing, Rothersthorpe

First published 2025

© Ricky Dale 2025

ISBN 978-1-78792-106-1

Book design, layout and production management by Into Print
www.intoprint.net
+44 (0)1604 832149

ACKNOWLEDGEMENTS

I am particularly grateful for the kindness, good company and pure professionalism of the folk who worked with me on this novel. My old ways and their more contemporary ways help to bring this novel and, indeed, my previous novels to fruition.

A to Z they are as follows:
  Social media manager – *Christelle Louise Shuttleworth*
  Montreal editor - *Dianne Letky*
  PC and typescript - *Jon Manley*
  Facsimile – *Peter Layland*
  Torquay Photo Centre – *Ras Virdee*

Special thanks to Paragon Publishing and Mark and Anne Webb for agreeing to publish this novel – moreover, for all the other novels they have published for me.

Last, and by no means least, thanks to my beloved daughter: Dr. Kimberley Jayne.

North America Email Reviews:

"Stark, rugged but so full of delights"
BOOK WORLD NEWS

"The characterisation of the hero/heroine are both rich and convincing"
NEW MILLENNIUM REVIEW

"Hilariously innocent and funny at times, though always on the brink of disaster!"
PACIFIC STORIES & POEMS

"Ricky Dale succeeds in transforming cynicism into a childlike vulnerability"
NEW ORLEANS REVIEW

"Doo-b'i on-ton-druh!
Only a Parisian woman would truly understand how the seducer can become the seduced!"
EVENING ARTS & LETTERS

Author Note

With reference to the poetry at the commencement of each chapter … In essence, the poems are simply intended as a 'warm-up act'[1] – for your enjoyment – indeed, they have no connection whatsoever to the story-line per se.

Kind regards
Ricky Dale

---

1   The author - an in-house singer – performed warm-up acts at the Brant Inn in Burlington, Ontario. The star singers might include folks such as Sophie Tucker, Ella Fitzgerald, Andy Williams, Johnnie Ray, Johnnie Mathis and Eartha Kitt.

Contents

Central Characters

Severine & Ricky...Singing duo
(AKA The Kowarsky Twins)

Carlos Marcello.................................Head honcho NY Mafia

Betty & Walter ....London landlady and son

Don Ceville .... Montreal Mafia

Reg & Ron Kray.................................London entrepreneurs
(AKA The Kray Twins)

George Raft .... Former movie star

Frances Kray .... Wife of Reg Kray

Sylvestro 'Silver Dollar' Sam Carollo...Montreal Mafia Boss
(Employer of Severine and Ricky)

Ruth Magdalene Minnelli .... Silvestro's whore

Mareille Balin ....Friend and good-time girl

Griselda Bianco .... Boss AKA Godmother

Aunt Helena..........................Guardian of Severine & Ricky
when children

Mike Bellisarious ....'Wild' brother of Severine & Ricky

Double Entendre

Peter Kowarsky .... Absent father of Ricky & Severine

Yvres Trudeau .... Hell's Angel

Diana Dors & Alan Lake .... British friends of Severine & Ricky

Katherine & Mathilda .... Singing duo and friends (AKA The Kerstin Sisters)

Prologue/Foreword

'Mafia' is now one of a long list of words – like 'pizza', 'spaghetti', 'opera' – that Italian has given to other languages across the world. It is commonly and inappropriately applied to criminals far beyond Sicily and the United States, which are the places where the Mafia, in the strict sense, is based. In other words, the term 'Mafia' has become an umbrella label for a whole panoply of gangs – Chinese, Japanese, Russian, Chechen, Albanian, Turkish, and so on – all of which have little or nothing to do with the original Mafia.

The media also use the word to describe loose confederations of people participating in some type of collective, unsavoury behaviour. Oftentimes we see and hear references to the financial Mafia, the waste-hauling Mafia, the political Mafia etc.

Countless films and novels have, indeed, helped to lend a sinister glamour to the Mafia. Mafia stories are always so compelling because they dramatize the everyday occurrences by adding hair-trigger thrills. It would be both pious and untrue to say that the Mafia presented in fiction is simply false; however, it is somewhat stylized. Among other things, Tommaso Buscetta distinguished himself as a contract killer. We spoke over dinner once and he told me how he was a fan of *The Godfather* movie. He said that he thought the scene at the end where other mafiosi kiss Michael Corleone's hand was unrealistic!

It does seem to me though that the conflicting demands that lie behind the motivation of a fictional character like Al Pacino's Michael Corleone – ambition, responsibility, family – are indeed the same ones that are central to the lives of real mafiosi.

There are countless bars, clubs and gaming establishments that are presided over or under absolute ownership of the 'Organization' (Mafia) or elusive modules of the same.

With that in mind our reader may be astonished to learn that my twin sister and yours truly were on the payroll of the 'Organization' and, indeed, its affiliates, for longer than we care to admit.

Our forte as a brother and sister act was singing our very own innovative approach to many traditional standards. Unlike other vocal duos such as Marvin Gaye and Tammi Terrell or Karen and Richard Carpenter, intimacy was the key to our sound. Southern Ontario and New York State were our current stomping grounds.

From time to time, Severine and Ricky have

ruminated on decamping from the music business totally. Perhaps establish a bona fide home – with all we are continuously on the road, living out of suitcases. We have some money to put by and so we could even consider an early retirement. However, what really freaks us out about our daydream is how are our bosses going to react at the thought of us being let loose?

The unwritten and accepted rule-book says that even innocently, you cannot take the inflammatory knowledge you have acquired with you when you absent yourself. In other words, you will be graveyard dead pretty damn quick!

'Singing' to Severine and Ricky was based upon highly acclaimed Broadway musicals and Sinatra, Tony Bennett, Richard Beymer and Natalie Wood, Elvis and more. 'Singing' has a special connotation in the world of gangsters. Singing like a 'canary' is a less-than-flattering term from the underworld lexicon of the day.

Yes, so it's true Severine and Ricky have, in fact, learned more than they themselves imagine. Such as a one-time remark from a professional hitter:

"… *after all, it's strictly business!*".

Ricky Dale's

1

Wilderness Crossing

What is love?
Love is where you
Take away lies
And substitute
For hope and trust,
Good strong coffee
And hot fresh baked
Apple pie!

Severine and Ricky feasted on apple pie à la mode during the greater part of their public performance in Wittenberg – just couldn't get enough of it!

This was every mom's and mother's sons' notion of classic apple pie to end all! Unknowingly simple mortals like us had been palmed off with tenth-rate apple pie for donkey's years, but this was at last the tantalizing pukka machismo of apple pie.

Crisp apples and sweet pastry that had taught entire generations of Martha Stewarts the way to folk's hearts, decades prior to lame technology getting its ambiguous clutch in our kitchens.

Steaming with pent-up energy, golden latticed plated and overall prodigious and voluminous delight; lifted out of the outworn stove by the most fetching and the bonniest gal imaginable; dressed in blue gingham; the natural complement to apple pie! *Eat whilst it's hot* the signage suggested and, in the subdued afternoon light, the byword was living up to its classic meaning.

Such a dinky, yet alert and active diner you couldn't imagine better. Cutlery clinked, skillets clanked whilst the pioneer frontiers-women scurried hurriedly to and fro from kitchen to diner with copious perks of freeze-dried coffee and cream.

Tragically the patriotic appeal was lost on the customers excepting the long-distance drivers who had a strong liking – indeed an appetite – for those curvaceous girls! The attention that had gone into giving this establishment a nostalgic frontier theme was, along with the apple pie, admirable although somewhat overindulgent: apologies to the cherished Davy Crockett for whatever inaccuracy.

> O beautiful for spacious skies,
> For amber waves of grain,
> For purple mountain majesties
> Above the fruited plain.

Had Katherine Lee Bates (1913) been waxing lyrical about wilderness crossing apple pie? Moreover, was Patrick Henry (1775) a patron demanding "Victuals, Liberty or Death"?

Remember this: it's actually apple pie that tends to make America great – not firearms; not the somewhat dreamy and far-sighted fantasist rubbernecking out toward the next horizon (or so).

In bluntly spoken English metrical verse, written by some humdrum benefactors, their take was as follows:

"It outwits copulation by and by, naught as enjoyable as mom's apple pie!"

2

Wittenberg

We would travel out of love –
If that way was any way but long
So tired of all the endless journeys
No, it seems more simple
And maybe more sure
Not to move even an iota

"Great songs and artists never really die – they just go on forever." So says my Severine – with aplomb too! "What, even in a unique place like Wittenberg?" yours truly cynically replied.

Wittenberg is a somewhat plutocratic entity both in its location, rich history and small-town charm. There is no question that it is blessed with its very own distinct and independent existence. Not only but also, nearby in the north woods of Wisconsin lies a Mohican resort offering the very best in Las Vegas style entertainment for all to squander their spondu-licks comprehensively and indiscriminately!

"I am in a quandary Ricky over the uncertainty of what's expected tonight. First-hand we were notified by the boss to run through songs for a cabaret, then recapitulated to a concert, last heard it's now a funeral party?"

Don't you be fretting little sister, I've got the whole shambolic ignominy sussed: all the ladies over 40 will be corseted and wrapped up to look like tutti-frutti dolls – the bad guys, of no redeeming qualities, will be tuxedoed – and the nasty flunkies will be suited and eating doner kebabs (in slices!).

It all worked out well-nigh OK in the end. It turned out that we had been requested to provide appropriate songs and music at a wake, where the deceased had departed in rather an abrupt manner. His friends and relatives had come together to see the late lamented on his way. Also, a host of folks that we didn't know turned up too – perhaps thinking that this was the concert or such! We'd crooned our way through much of the same gatherings many times in the past – so as far as our duties were concerned it was ditto!

Severine and I put on our most melancholy faces and, during the recess, we casually meandered over to the spread where she was tearfully sat. Apparently, she was the matriarch and so I respectfully enquired "How'd he die ma'am?" She'd stopped boohooing now and, in a run-of-the-mill lack of concern, she replied: "Two bullets to the back of his head".

As we walked back to the stage, Severine whispered to me: "Welcome to Little Sicily Ricky!"

3

God Ranks

I've been to town.
Walked the highways and the
harbours too
done some things I thought I'd
never do.
You ask me why it is
I frown.
I guess it's just because
I've been to town.

I've been to town.
Beyond the boulevards
and beach.
I've learned things only time
can teach:
that love is more than just
a speech.
It's got to find some
common ground
I know this because
I've been to town.

The power of the Camorra – mainland Italy's version of the Sicilian Mafia – is far more appreciable than that of other Mafia crime groups. Inasmuch that they oftentimes act totally independently – even of one another. For this reason, it makes them more resilient when things go-pear-shaped. For example, when top leaders are arrested or killed, new dons often emerge from the remnants of the old ones.

Severine and yours truly have worked and socialized with the Organization – from the bosses to the 'mechanics' – for over a decade, and in all that time we are still unable to fully comprehend all of the why and wherefores of their 'secret society' per se. Severine once concluded that: "Only God is the centrepiece in the making of a good Camorrista, by virtue of his high rank!"

Taking a break, between numbers and peering out from the wings across the stage and down onto the dance floor proper, has its own 'reverence' of a kind. For example, I couldn't help to notice that the dear departed guy's old lady looked far from grieved. Perhaps she was merely a resilient old hen, but canoodling with the dead guy's son was a senseless time-out. In any event, it was just a matter of time before she was escorted off the dance floor by a solid burly guy in an ill-fitting tux. By the grace and courtesy of our host she would most likely be chauffeured home, however, if she decides to cause a kick-off, at worse she may accidentally fall from the balcony!

It seems to me that hovering in the background of certain folk's minds are insistent voices telling them that lies and inexcusable conduct are tolerable for the well-to-do. That's how it was with the dead guy's chick!

4

Purple Chrysanthemums

My twin
is the friend I dreamed
of finding.
She transcends gender,
eliminates cold September
and adds another month
of Sundays
to my well-worn calendar

Severine was the 'boss' who applied the tanned 'smear' to our observable theatrical parts, just prior to our opening. Habitually, in time-honoured fashion, suits of black plush velour were always the directive (resembling velvet, but less expensive). Me being 40 minutes Severine's senior, my long-time twin and I had been implementing our act together for so many donkey's years that we had developed our own very particular 'horse' sense. Fuss and palaver rehearsals with regard to the others' musical interpretation of a certain number, were ever so and indeed comparatively rare.

It's kind of both cute and somewhat sanctimonious too when you know each other's habits so very thoroughly – not only the highly sophisticated on-stage façade they have adopted, but also from a subjective personal standpoint too. Indeed, my sister is a goody-goody, somewhat prissy and wholeheartedly pernickety blonde hellcat, and if you imagine that the colour of her hair is not at all relevant to the subject matter in question – I can assure your good self it indubitably is!

A typical evening would find my comatose mind imbued with a false sense of purpose, crooning off-by-heart lyrics, whilst Severine warbles along a succession of time-worn non-mindfulness.

Our Sicilian bosses and doting throng swallow up with obvious pleasure and The Royal Bank of Canada was enthused too.

At the end of the evening a head honcho – Carlos Marcello – would present my Severine with time-honoured, (finest pick) purple chrysanthemums; his preferred choice!

5

Blighty

*Genius consists of its
powers of reflection
and not of the intrinsic
quality of the performance.*

It seemed to us that the clubs were the intrinsic part of the nightlife – not as a matter of course the singer/song!

Just recently both Severine and me are not sleeping as well as we should be. Bizarre things happen when we doze off. It's as though we have become involved in another life, which to all intents and purposes is very similar to ours except that we are seeing it through an eavesdrop and cannot escape. Severine says that she becomes the go-between, a messenger between two worlds, which is similar to what I too experience. In fact, there doesn't seem to be any variation in our individual dreams – the facts between us are the same, viz: the man with the rifle looking through binoculars so leisurely at mothers and their babies playing. And then a strange mishmash of different things and different people: grandmothers knitting the news; housewives on their Christmas shopping sprees; soldiers on their manoeuvres. The only possible enemy – the suited man with binoculars and hunting rifle.

*

I awaken; Severine awakens too – beside me boohooing. We had again gained access to each other's enumerate nocturnal demons and stretched each one to fluorescence. "Read me Walt Whitman dear Ricky – I need to listen to his honest innocence; we need innocence Ricky." I put in my two cents: "We need diversity little sister, that's why we're scheduled on a flight to Blighty at 2.45pm today – it's across the pond for us sis."

6

The Contract

I need from you:
suspension –
– absolution of a kind.

I need from you:
A now –
– That turns into an always

But first some rethink time:

I need from you:
Free and so freely –
– the way we pretend we are.

And so it came to pass that after a decade of press, paparazzi and threats to our sanity, we'd received the purple chrysanthemums for the final time. From Portland, Maine, to Portland, Oregon, and indeed Portofino harbour, the mechanism that propelled us and encroached upon our private relationships had called it quits. The erroneous age where being a desirable act is not the be-all and end-all had finally become outstretched once and for all.

However, what disturbed us was primarily that folks on the Organization payroll seldom, if ever, take a leave of permanent absence of their own volition. Indeed, we are not aware of any person or people who have established a bona fide alternative, although it's impossible to be absolutely certain.

We knew, and naturally enough, the powers-that-be knew about Mafia activities. Our indifferent and bland attitude to such shenanigans made us popular and well-liked, however, would they now consider our alliance put in jeopardy by the slim probability that we were to betray their trust – or put another way 'rat them out'!

Invocation:
It may indeed happen
that in some hidden middle night
you'll rise up
and come to me
in solitude or silence.

We will meet
as we have met
on a train, or at the end
of some new train of thought.

Me, blue-jeaned and apple-cheeked
you, freckled, smiling
like a China cup
over blue and white gingham.

7

To Be or Not?

There is a common refrain among academics and law enforcement officials more often than not. Those of them who have studied the Italian Mafia stringently agree that, in many ways, they are the seed group for all other crime syndicates. Perhaps arguably, but the true way to fully understand Mafia 'law', is first and foremost you must understand 'Sicily'.

*

Editor's footnote: Severine and Ricky have been enjoying their lives in a country not drawn on any map. A domain that is both aloof and austere to outsiders, yet at the same time appear friendly and likeable. The mistaken belief that, after a decade of eating from the same bowl, Severine and Ricky don't consider themselves surplus to requirements leaves me gob-smacked!

Severine/Ricky footnote: Tittle-tattle backstage knew of our intention to jack-in. Apparently there had been an attempt to slip us a 'mickey', however insightful members of the band thwarted it!

8

Hilariously Innocent and Diverse

The time we take to say:
"I love you"
is all that we need
at the outset of our days

Can there really be such a thing as platonic love? An innocent non-physical, perhaps even spiritual love. Yeah, there most certainly can be, particularly when the persons in question are twins who have been parted for most of their lives. Of course, the passers-by took no heed to the impassioned couple (us) enveloped in a snuggle, however the tide would be turned had they known said couple's parallel bond!

In any event it was 'welcome to London, England'; it's almost offensive hubbub, smoke grimed atmosphere from a thousand fireplace chimneys and the repetitive snazzy flashing from the neons, all power for the course!

A little old dwarfed newspaper vendor yelled at me "Evening Herald Yanks?" Had we really inadvertently already assumed a North American swagger or some such?

No matter how long you are out of the country, those corner, little simplistic fag shops seem to endure. No stateside smokes though – seems as if we are going to be puffing on Woodbines or Weights for the foreseeable future!

The wet behind the ears counter assistant (poor kid) was getting mighty confused over the issue of sugar coupons and cigarette coupons. To lighten the load on her I casually quipped "One's a handicap on the belly, the other is a handicap on the lungs". She didn't react but, ultimately, she asked for my identity card and duly showed me where to sign.

Whilst the assistant rang up our change, my Severine melted her lipstick on two Player's Weights and sprang the Zippo into action. The crossfire of our glances indicated that it was fun to be back in dear old Blighty again – the bitterly cold shop, the exploited youngster – nothing really changes!

We stepped out into the inhospitable cold-hearted night. The bitterness seemed to just cling to your clothes. Severine took an impetuous inhale from her fag and commented: "I wouldn't imagine that Maf is stalking us this evening, what with the time difference and all, it's still lunchtime stateside". I half-heartedly smiled at her: "Yeah, most probably they have been much too dispassionate to even notice our absence".

Severine was oftentimes in one of her odd philosophically quirky moods at certain times of the month! When this 'metamorphosis' kicked-off it was my prerogative to attempt to figure out where her engaging tête-à-tête was coming from and indeed where it was going!

At that precise period in time, we were both sauntering arm-in-arm down this foggy never-ending London street, when sis all of a sudden anxiously announced: "Half of me sets my heart on us being hypothetical deceased – murdered or otherwise. However, the other half of me wishes for the rebirth of our souls in a new body". Knowingly but with somewhat disquiet I responded: "Time will heal sis, you'll see". She glanced at me with that super fanciful half smile of hers ... "Ricky we shouldn't under-estimate our adversaries' total unpredictability in such matters as this. In London folks expect: fish & chips – cup o' tea – bad food – worse weather – Mary Fuckin' Poppins – but not Cosa Nostra Ricky, not Cosa Nostra. Londoners are unschooled presently; in a short time, they will be though."

Suddenly and somewhat unexpectedly and obscure edifice of grimy stone emerged from out of the grey fog. Severine pointed her brolly excitedly:

"It's a boarding house Ricky, with a fuckin' vacancy sign too!" In a sloping typeface in the window it read *Bed and breakfast offered to paying guests.*

Ricky Dale's

In the pre-dawn hours
lying together
all arms and legs
and breathing
and the morning rain
far away
and the morning is coming

I hoped never to see the sun again
and now ...
your face and the sun
making this room
with ceiling sky
in avenues of sunlit dust
beautiful
for us.

9

Crystalized in Time

The potted palm sitting sedately in the hallway, the stucco walls from an exhausted past of long age. The pale and tired semi-conscious banquet, chairs propping open doors of vacant rooms; and the beguiling octogenarian landlady with a faithful Bow Bells dialect. "Care for a sarnie and cocoa to take up to bed with you?" she asked and carried on: "O lovers, lovers, I knew you were sweethearts just as soon as you walked in. My husband was a 'lover', he's over there." She nodded in the direction of an earthenware pot … "divine love handles he had too".

She chaperoned us to our room and wished us "sleep tight, don't let the bed bugs bite", which I hoped was a polite euphemism of sorts! We 'flushed' the sarnies but endured the cocoa – at least it was hot and wet! Severine and yours truly agreed that we had spent worse Sunday evenings but couldn't remember where!

In a world that is constantly evolving – our world

in particular – the utopia of having each other was mighty gratifying. For her sins, so was Betty our landlady. "In love, ah in love" she got that one partially right, except that only sister and brother know what it's like to discover a natural awareness and all its ebullience too.

The abominable lavatory and other ablutions were situated up some steep stairs on the third floor. For the purpose of a quick jimmy riddle it was perhaps bearable; however, when it became my Severine's turn in completing her task, she exited like a ballerina who'd stubbed her toe, even before she'd removed her undies: "It's stinky, unhygienic and filthy Ricky and I'm never setting foot in that cesspool again" … she really meant it too! And so it came to pass that my sis, Miss Prim & Proper, took to peeing in our bedroom wash basin! It was indeed a sight and moments to behold! Not merely on account of my sanctimonious schoolmarmish sister with a holier-than-thou attitude toward respectability had fallen by the wayside – by peeing in the sink – but moreover, the fact that her pernicketyness and self-importance had eventually gotten the better of her prissiness!

After all of the many years and circumstances of annoyance we had engaged in, it was nevertheless a challenge for me not to feel more than rousing sympathy each and every occasion my sister took a pee! To call to mind a person of such explicit handsomeness, positioning her bonny and somewhat bony derriere above our bedroom wash basin, still leaves me ruffled – attractive and appealing in appearance; she was not a prepossessing sight!

The 'crummy' for quality B&B which was to become the home from home for Severine and yours truly for an unknown length of time, did still have its advantages though. Apart from us two having a silly soft spot for Betty, and her dopey, dippy ways, the tarnished B&B was situated somewhat virtuously just across the street from a spotless Sally Army institution. For the princely sum of two shillings and six pence each, we'd accommodate a double bathroom with lashings of hot water too, for however long we wished. On the odd occasion we'd bring the transistor and listen to *Woman's Hour*. Although brother and sister, there was still a magic about bathing side by side. We've crooned the Sammy Cahn and Jimmy Van Heusen number many times: "...*you can't have one without the other*".

In addition to that good news, we'd found a haberdasher who sells this newfangled 'foam'. We purchased a piece around the size of a cushion, cut out the middle and hey presto success – it acts as a buffer against the porcelain wash basin and Severine's curvaceous but bony bottom!

10

Love is in Hyde Park

In Hyde Park
Lovers don't hide
Thinkers stroll
And dreamers wander
Side by Side.

In Hyde Park
Lovers lie and lie
Entwined upon the grass
Visible and yet unseen
By the others strolling by
Beneath the leafy green.

In Hyde Park
Though no wall or tree may hide,
Lovers live their lives apart,
Locked in the privacy of the human heart.

In Hyde Park
Lovers lie
And lie

Ricky Dale's

O lovers, lovers
Clasp the moment to your breasts
And you, the others passing by
Turn away the peering eye
Leave them loving on the grass
Love — like summer
All too soon must pass.

11

Fib of Vision

The dandelion
hasn't yet been known
to make
its choice between
the pasture
and the lawn ...
... and neither have I!

In a cupboard, in a shed, at the bottom of Betty's back yard, is a pair of leather Italian dancing shoes. Every now and then, Betty takes them out of the cupboard and gives them a jolly good dubbin; especially for softening and waterproofing expensive leather. This procedure is all in preparedness of her son's arrival. He is a hard-working bloke called Walter who treasures the shoes which were gifted to him by an Italian POW for assistance in relocating same to the UK.

The POW's name was Gennaro Panzuto and, unfortunately, he has since passed on. However, fortnightly, whenever there is a 'U' in the month, Walter can be found spinning across the neighbourhood palais dance floor in his gifted real leather dancing shoes.

Walter is normally an unpretentious and unassuming individual whose claim to fame is trying to grow pots of basil on his wind-swept, rented (2/6 per week), allotment patch for umpteen years. However, fast forward to fortnightly Saturdays (whenever there is a 'U' in the month) and he transforms into a gregarious, charismatic and somewhat arrogant Italian stud. Sexually desirable too; some say! (Recounted by a friend who wishes to remain anonymous).

In wintertime England of the 1950s, it's a big advantage to assume your living abode is warm and cosy when, in fact, it's not unlike living in a shed … "simulated make-believe" it's called. With that in mind, Severine and I were dead set on treading the boards at the local palais Walter had sung his praises about, if only to keep warm! He was keen to introduce us "his American friends" to his dancing cohorts too. The East London palais smelled of Brussel sprouts, farts and a hint of Old Spice aftershave. A heavily built beefy man, with silvery hair and moustache, greeted us and escorted us to a cute little table on the edge of the dance floor. "I was wondering when you'd decide to visit our humble establishment" he said. Looking across the floor at a regular couple who had just seated themselves at an adjoining table he remarked naffly "We rarely have the pleasure of truly talented stars from across the pond, here at the palais, do we?"

Unless Walter's dancing shoes had a hotline installed to the Camorra, we felt reasonably out of danger and secure in the fact that our names were not going to be written in blood at Bethnal Green palais this evening – perhaps on the streets of Naples though, but we are not there! We had learned a lot regarding the Hollywood stereotype where the all-powerful family tend to control an entire city or even some far-fetched country. We had learned first-hand that the true flexibility and the true fluidity of the Camorra lays principally in its power to recruit smaller clans. Seems to me, via the resplendent rumours from the grapevine, that right here in dear old Blighty, more is to be feared by some up and coming guys from Bethnal Green though!

It's the little things I remember most:
The left turn
you attempted on a red light.
The cool air,
as we ventured out on a summer evening.
The enjoyment of breakfast together
– coffee and hot donuts.
Your naked back,
to cuddle up to at night.
The British subway,
so new and exciting to us.
The buskers, the music,
that seemed to last forever.
The erotic kiss to say goodnight
and the smooching in spite of it!

12

Each To Their Own

The underworld has always been attracted to show business folk, except in the case of Severine and Ricky the so-called attraction had become a controlling obsession by the powers that be. We'd worked as solo acts for years but, as a couple, were not nearly so well known in the UK club circuit as we were in North America. Although perhaps things changed for the better that winter evening after Severine and Ricky did their own rendition of the 1942 Harold Arlen and Johnny Mercer classic *That Old Black Magic* … by request of the Bethnal Green Palais management.

I suppose that, in many respects, Severine and yours truly were, depending upon which way you look at it, a little over naïve regarding gangsters and their high society associates. However, it had come to our attention, via Betty, that Don Ceville from the Canadian Mafia was, at present, swaggering around London Town hoping to do business. Dear Betty encouraged us to keep hushed – but we did not heed her advice! We wrongly assumed that America was America and England was England and never the twain shall meet, a very childlike presumption that, in due course, may be rebutted!

The bottom line was that we couldn't go indefinitely using our credit card, we needed to get back to work, and so we were delighted when Walter told us he had fixed us an interview at the Double R Club in Bow Road, which wasn't too far away. Reg and Ron Kray, or "The Kray Twins", as they were known, not only booked us at the new Double R Club but also at the rather high-class Kentucky Club on Saturday Nights.

We became very friendly with the Double Rs. I had a feeling that they were aware of our background and, in their own ways, they were 'watching our backs'. I once remarked to my Severine that in the event some Organization shooter from stateside was to come looking for us on Double R (Kray) territory, I think that Reg and Ron would preserve the status quo in no uncertain terms!

Rightly or wrongly so, it seemed to me that because Severine and I were also twins like their esteemed selves, that perhaps there was somehow a connection in our joint narrative of notions? We were all at the bar one evening when Reg madly made a saucy assertion with reference to our 'tackle', viz: "Twins you are but your tackle differs Sev!"

During our break one evening, who should walk across to the bar but the legendary movie king of gangsters, the man himself George Raft. As a youngster I had watched him play the ambitious and nearly insane killer in so many movies and I loved him to bits: *Scarface*, *Rogue Cop* and even *Some Like It Hot*. I so admired his work. He was aged in his early 70s then, and I have never seen a more smartly dressed 'hood'!

Several years later we became close friends and I asked him, somewhat cheekily, where his longevity came from. He confided that he allowed himself just one meal per day which consisted of a steak with salad at 7pm every evening. He said he never smoked or drank at all. Shortly before his death he presented Severine and me with a gold-plated Zippo lighter, each engraved G. Raft. He had always been a highly regarded actor and a unique man and friend too.

Pretty soon they replaced us at the Double R and we were working seven nights per week at the more prestigious and highly regarded Kentucky Club. It was undoubtedly the uppermost point for all celebrities, including regulars such as Roger Moore and Lord Snowden to name just two.

By today's standards the Kentucky Club was probably somewhat loud and garish. Deep red carpets, tinted wall-to-ceiling plate glass mirrors and sprayed gold 'antique' chairs and furniture. However, the Kentucky Club was spot on right for its times. More especially, it was right for the toffs who wanted to come across from the West End and see for themselves a bit of the seamy side of life, without having to get themselves dirty, or put themselves in any undue danger.

The toffs loved it. It was exciting; it was exhilarating. They could kid themselves it was dangerous because there were plenty of evil-looking so-called gangsters around – like our dear George Raft!

Not only but also, the club provided many gaming tables and sophisticated entertainment too – us! There were oftentimes some novel types of entertainment too, which those ineffectual hooray Henrys could go home to their pad and tell their hoity-toity friends about it too.

One of the stage acts frequently used was called "Tex the Dwarf". He was a midget who wore an enormous Texan style hat. He would often climb onto the back of a (real) donkey and strum away on a guitar and sing cowboy songs. At the end of the act Reg or Ron would walk up onto the stage and lead the donkey over to the bar by its reins and give it a large glass of gin and tonic as its treat!

The police were in and out of the club – more

often than a wholesome hooker – keeping an eye on everybody's interests including their own! Eventually though all good times come to an end and a new DI closed the popular Kentucky Club down. Ron said it was blatant persecution and not being able to read between the lines. Severine and yours truly were inclined to agree with him.

I'll never understand the reason why but after the penultimate interim raid, Severine and I were locked in the cells overnight. Afterwards when we were released Severine declared: "At least we were safe from Don Ceville (Canadian Mafia) perhaps being held in custody was a benediction of sorts" … Severine had a catholic education!

13

Nice Girls Don't Stay For Breakfast

Severine and I kept a day-to-day journal of events during our UK visit. From the onset we had no intention of recording and thereby revealing the special relationship that we enjoyed as friends of Ron and Reg Kray. We were both of accord – Severine and I – that in any event personal detail should be kept separate from the main story per se. With somewhat mixed feelings we've told of our salubrious days with them and trust that this connection is acceptable to their living friends and family.

It seems to me that, at this point in our story, it's worth pointing out that we believe that the guys had something of a soft spot for Severine and me, and we still cannot imagine them being involved in gangland killings and such. Sorry if our naivety is somewhat difficult for the reader to comprehend – we can only speak as we found.

Perhaps the additional most positive tick in all of our favours is the unique and lovely Frances Shea. Frances was pure and innocent – the body of a woman with a sweet mind of a child. She was Reg's girl and as such she brought a wonderful sort of simplicity into Reg's life. He fell for her big time and it was noticeable to us how he changed. Frances had been our Severine's girlfriend for some time and eventually one evening at the Double R club, Severine introduced her to Reg.

It was like he was 18 again. Oftentimes you'd see them in a pub enjoying a gin and tonic together. They would play this strange game together – I still can't fathom out the rules – he'd get a heap of coins from behind the bar and ask her to name the East End slang names for each of the coins. For example: a half-crown (2 shillings and 6 pence) was a "tosheroon"; 5 shillings was a "caser"; 5 pounds was a "jack"; and so on. Every time Frances remembered the name correctly, he would empty the money into her little handbag.

Severine said that Frances was an old-fashioned decent sort of girl – the way that Reg 'liked'. Although their marriage didn't prevent her death at only 23 years of age. We had been to their East End wedding just a couple of years previously, it was really a fairy tale event. We'd heard that Reg was broken when she died. Unfortunately, we were back in America by that time with many unresolved uncertainties to face off.

14

We Read and Sing Aloud

We read and sing aloud
first Cohen then Eliot
twenty stanzas at a time
your turn, then mine.
I raise my eyes to admire your body
and stumble as usual in mid-metaphor
of exasperation and irritation.

We leave our sitting room
turn off the porch light and
pausing near the window
We hold one another until,
until we reach the kitchen
and make love on the table –
– the hard wood floor too.

Your cheeks now smell
like lemon.
We roll we bump
against the converse cupboards.
I carry you to bed.
I marry you in your night clothes –
– all in the turquoise light of eternity.

15

The Montreal Connection - Part 1

Some songs do not exist
They become absent
without the singer.
Certain rhymes are trapped
and become lost
in their own pages.
These are the things we know
about songs,
about rhymes,
and yet real eternal magic
will rampage only
from the inside
to the outside
of all eternal things.

Fire, rivers; plum and cherry blossom:
such visions of vigilance.
The dreamer, the traveller:
has carried back from worlds apart.
Me … I only worry over the absence
of you whom I love.

16

The Montreal Connection - Part 2

The ultimate destination for Severine and Ricky was their homeland, Canada: moreover, it was our darling Montreal, Canada's Mafia capital.

Montreal was blessed with a large hard-working immigrant population of French-speaking Italian folk on one hand. On the other hand, the French-speaking province of Quebec, in general, was also a natural home-from-home refuge for French and Corsican gangsters from Marseilles. It also embraced its own Mafia family which was allied to families in New York.

The Camorrista clan who Severine and Ricky had been involved with as entertainers, acted with completely independency of the Montreal Mafia, indeed there wasn't any love lost between the two clans. With that in mind, we reasoned that by us cutting ties with our old 'employer' the Camorra, might actually put us in good stead with the Montreal family. As luck had it, what clinched us coming to work for the so-called 'good guys' was that during the fall of 1979 a hugely important, and therefore elaborate, wedding was being held at the rather affluent Hotel Pierre in New York and many major figures from the Canadian, American and Sicilian clans would be attending as guests. It's perhaps worth mentioning that certain relatives of the late and respected Carlo Gambino were invited too.

I think that everyone knows that 'singing' has a special connotation to many Italian folk and people in general, especially at ceremonies such as weddings. There is the somewhat literal hint in Mafia circles 'to sing like a canary'. This less than flattering term indicates that the 'canary' as such is likely to take a header from a tenth-floor window – or such![2] However, singing the Sinatra and Bennett way is to be adored by all!

With regard to the forthcoming wedding, the powers that be decided upon using the music and lyrics that Sammy Cahn composed for *Robin and the 7 Hoods*; they said it would be apt and seemly amusing too: *My Kind of Town / Luck Be A Lady*, but moreover the lucky bride was genuinely called Marion! And so it came to pass: from London, England to Montreal, Canada – all in one 'foul swoop'!

Severine and I spent several days searching for an

---

2   Following the demise of a certain 'canary', it was mentioned regarding his present status that "he could sing but he couldn't fly"!

apartment whilst, during the interim, we stayed at the reasonably priced Hotel de Paris in the French quarter. It was becoming financially crucial that we returned to work.

Eventually we discovered the perfect apartment. It was in a condominium just one street east of the Outremont area and very close to the club. The apartment was, by any standards, very spacious – long corridors, high ceilings and with a balcony that overlooked the street below. "Somewhat a contrast to that Bethnal Green dump" Severine remarked with a hint of well-founded sarcasm. "Yeah, and you don't have to pee in the wash basin" I retorted thankfully!

The streets of Outremont seemed to be packed to teeming with past and present celebrities. Severine was 'again' tugging on my coat sleeve because she thought she saw Pierre Trudeau. "Still so suave, even in his seventies" she excitedly exclaimed. Me … I was just wanting in need of coming across the great master of us all and king of cool, the incomparable Mr Leonard Cohen! It was meltdown for us after the over-dramatic goings-on and jiggery-pokery of the past year.

*

Now in our niche apartment we spent the greater part of our days glancing through the entertainment listings in the Montreal Central Library, or running through trial performances – dry runs were our forte. All of our dates and times were now arranged and confirmed – we missed the public gaze and it was fabulous to be back, doing what we did best.

17

Mareille Balin

Bare-chested
coming from the bathroom –
– she looked like every invitation
that I'd ever dreamed of
that never came true.
I salute
the sensibility of your
adorable nakedness
and pledge my allegiance to it
as my only true
place of residence!

Our chance meeting with Mareille at Maisonneuve Market was, upon reflection, an unholy titillating occurrence. "Oh, come on," she said over our inability to choose a soft or hard watermelon! That smouldering voice, that piercing gaze, those towering cheek bones put me in mind of a Hepburn woman (Katherine – absolutely not Audrey!). I couldn't make up my mind though and still unsure as yet, whether she is super-cool or merely icy?

By all accounts we were neighbours, at least we owned apartments in the same condominium. That's where the similarity ended! Mareille Balin used her apartment jointly with a couple of others – although the so-called 'others' were not at all aware of the bizarre arrangement per se! On the one hand, she was supposedly the beautiful mistress of a Parisian politico, however more openly, so was the authorized aficionado to writer François Truffaut.

I knew that Severine was indeed bi-curious and, as for yours truly, 'judgemental' was the equivalent to a word from a foreign or alien country. And so, with that in mind we three arranged to enjoy coffee and cakes at Le Commensal that very afternoon, for some 'conferring'.

I guess we all learned a smidgen of forthrightness that atypical afternoon together. In Mareille's world being 'bi' is not at all as challenging as you may think … "providing you are comprehensively right-minded toward yourself and the person who you are partaking any type of activity with." She clarified by adding "when I was a teenager I wanted to 'come out' to my parents – they were fascinated but apparently they already had a hunch – so that part went really well. Next on the list was my boyfriend at the time who remarked: "It doesn't matter a pig's ear to me". That part went really well too because it's all about you being right-minded to them and yourself too!"

Mareille went into some deep conversation with my Severine whilst I went to the counter and ordered more coffee. I have to admit I absorbed a lot of what she said and it really intrigues me a lot.

By the time I returned with our coffee the tête-à-tête was slowing somewhat and so I decided to throw in my two-penny worth of wisdom, as follows:

"Mareille my dear, do you ever feel it's less hard to wake up feeling lonely when you are alone, than wake up feeling lonely when you are with someone – male or female, would there be a difference?" "Have you been there Ricky?" she quizzed. So I quizzed her back. "Not recently, however I'm fortunate because I have my Severine. Here's a question that alludes me, I am only able to answer half because of me not being bi – whereas you may be able to answer both, dear Mareille. What about the moment of *desire*? What about when you know that something is about to happen? Do you not feel some kind of preference for male or female, dear Mareille?" "That is an excellent observation Ricky darling" she replied, in a quasi-divine tone: "that most exalting moment Ricky, be it male or female is absolutely inconsequential – here nor there, copiousness a 'gogo' is the only related link" … Severine, out of the blue, cut in – "right-mindedness too" she emphasized.

Later that afternoon when Mareille had headed off home, Severine and I sat for a while on a park bench and kind of blew some of our own thoughts into the hysteric mixture – Severine spoke first: "Fundamentally, I think that all women, young, or not so young, have an inherent elegance about them. Seems to me that in some respects that elegance is destroyed when they feel obliged to take off their clothes. I guess I never really thought of myself as some kind of sex guru as Mareille does – in fact I was never so happy as when I was miserable between love affairs. How about you Ricky? Before I went on my last date, it was sex I wanted and then we met and all of a sudden I wanted kisses and candlelight – that sort of thing, and sex too, I guess!"

18

Buttoned or Half Open

Don't tell me I'm beautiful
and lots of other lies
just hold me close and fuck me
with those simplistic sighs
and when it's finally over
make as if your love is true
there have been so many others lie
so there might as well be you!

It was around 7pm and the night outside was
sweltering at 90°F as only July in Montreal can be.
The doorbell rang almost tentatively and there on the
doorstep was our new buddy and pal Mareille, with a
look on her face like she'd wet her PJs! "Are you both
alone?" she enquired, "because I'd like to introduce
you to someone or rather I'd like 'someone' to be
introduced to me!" And then she just surges off on
a tangent of a completely different line of thought
– of strange investigative nondescript sentences
moulding into an amazingly long paragraph … not
unlike this one!

"Have you eaten yet? Do you approve of my new minidress? Have you had sex tonight? Amend that, you're twins, aren't you?" She was gushing now, but we didn't care one iota, not one shred! We couldn't help but adore our new found playmate: so sheepishly virtuous, so chaste, so pure and, in spite of all that, so sluttish!

She had obviously spied Severine and I purchasing two paintings from a market trader – and they are still tied back-to-back on our sideboard.

"Please Ricky, please Severine, I would be eternally grateful if you both could see fit to introduce me to that artist and, moreover, his partner too. Perhaps mention that I am a single girl and that you and I are long standing friends."

Severine looked Mareille amusingly in the eye: "Dear Mareille, we don't know that couple from Adam and Eve they are purely pedlars, traveling street traders. They were sat on the sidewalk selling paintings and we bought a couple, period!"

"Oh, you are both so *bourgeois*" she declared. "Severine, he and his partner both eat at Le Commensal on Rue St Denis – the self-same restaurant as *us*! Ricky, please *please*, sweet talk your Severine. I promise faithfully to keep my blouse buttoned up, or at the very most, half open only!"

Severine and I were suckers – five star! The 90°

apartment, the tentative doorbell and the 'artist et al'! How could we possibly spurn, nay rebuff, our little femme fatale – we couldn't! And so, with all of that running through our heads, the three of us eventually set out for supper at Le Commensal – we'd none of us eaten. To all intents and purposes, it was as though the evening at Le Commensal had been preordained because sat on a stool next to us, at the bar, was the tendentious couple: him with a brush behind his ear and his lady love dragging on a slim panatela like it was an elixir of sorts.

Mareille[3], completely unexpectedly, without an inch of prior warning, swivelled around on her stool to face them, and speaking in a low voice over her shoulder to us she murmured her intentions: "Don't be angry but not interested in the flabby painter, physically it's his fancy lady".

Without so much as a boo to a goose, Mareille's resourcefulness had taken her across the lounge to the bar steward and she'd arranged for a tray of

---

3   Apparently, she is a Newfoundland girl – originally. She explained to us that Newfoundland folk are not at all shy with regard to mentioning their liking of sex. In fact, there is nothing you can't discuss in Newfoundland when it comes to sex. It's natural enough to call up strangers and say "Hi, we're taking a survey and want to talk to you about sex: do you like sex? How much do you like sex? How often do you have sex?" However, do not talk about 'love', that makes Newfoundland folk very uncomfortable!

drinks for her new found intimates. Last we noticed was the victorious wink she gave us on the way out. Mademoiselle is nothing but formidable!

19

"I'll Keep My Arms Spread Wide"

I'll keep my arms spread wide
on a tightrope teetered.
Stretched between us
and your sometimes need for me
by my all-times need for you.

Balancing:
always balancing.
One foot
and then the other.
Down …
the roads and rails.
Across …
the stages and scenery.

Le Stage Dinner Theatre on Blvd Decarie was to be our venue Wednesdays through Sundays. Unquestionably an upgrade from the Double R Club and the aristocratic Kentucky Club too. Less hours and days to grapple with really suited us as well. Also, because of our British interrelationship, out international status had been raised as well.

The wireless was still popular in those days and, with time on our hands, Severine and I became quite ardent radio aficionados, which helped to give us more understanding and insight into what was currently sought after musically.

It's ironic how things can often happen in the opposite way to what is expected. In the comparatively short time that Severine and I were in the UK, a new generation of music lovers had begun to emerge in North America. It's sad to see how even some music legends had dissolved their acts. Seems to me that Severine and yours truly were fortunate to be on the cabaret circuit where things were – how shall I say – 'preserved'.

20

The Gang That Couldn't Shoot Straight

I'll teach you music
slowly and without pain.
And you can show me
how to make quiche Lorraine.

Le Stage Dinner Theatre in Montreal and Wilderness Crossing in Wittenberg have very little in common, outside of the fact that they are both controlled by Mafia families.

Our current gaffer at Le Stage is Sylvestro – 'Silver Dollar Sam' – Carollo. Sylvestro is also involved with assisting in the top management of other clubs, gambling enterprises, plus organized crime in general throughout Quebec. Several years previous to him becoming such a big shot, he had wed Nicole Binoche, a lady of reputable standing, inasmuch that she was the Provincial Postmaster's daughter in Laval, Quebec. Somewhat of a wise move by Sylvestro, because in marrying a local girl it had given him an air of much-needed respectability.

The so-called fairer sex had, in an indirect way, been Sylvestro's good fortune. Of late, his First Lieutenant is the notorious Griselda Bianco, variously known as "Mama Coca" and "La Madrina" (The Godmother). Despite her somewhat overt bisexuality, our dear Bianco had been married three times and allegedly killed all three husbands, pronto! Thus, earning her another nickname around town, viz: 'The Black Widow'.

Mercifully, Severine and yours truly were looked upon by our compatriots with an almost admiring reverence. Our links with the Camorrista (who as far as we know are still out for our blood) together with the Kray twins (their notoriety is now front-page news) has done much to enhance our profile as was, 'merely entertainers'.

On our rest days at home, it became customary to receive delivery of food and wine from various best-known restaurants and delicatessens across the city (Mafia owned). I said to Severine that there was no reason for us to be cynical, it's purely because our boss has decided to take us under his ample wings. Withall, he does enjoy a billionaire-dollar empire and even the Mafia is capable and certainly skilful enough to undergo a transmogrification!

"She's a biker's dream girl – 21 and she can suck-start a Harley" (unsigned).

One particular guy who fairly surprisingly would come to listen to our 'croon' at Le Stage was Quebec native Yvres Trudeau. He was a regular 'fan' who was around his early 30s and had a different girl on his arm each and every time! Yvres organized the Quebec chapter of the Hell's Angels motorcycle club. Just via the grapevine as such, he was known as a veteran killer! The first Canadian to wear a 'Filthy Few' patch on his vest, indicating that he was a biker who had murdered for the club.

One evening in conversation with him between performances he handed me my own 'Angels' patch as a gift. Said he admired our "hokey music". Said he was listening to it on the radio the night he executed three renegade Angels into the St Lawrence River.

When Severine and I were kids our Mom gave us some affirmative advice, viz: "Keep in with the bad folk and the good folk won't hurt you!"

21

Yonge Street Strip

Frightened …
at being alone
without you.
When the alternative is,
being with just anyone.
… that's something I don't
really need!

Sylvestro would 'lend' us out from time to time – typically with interest I expect!

Saint Jean Baptiste (June 24) is Quebec's national holiday, so Sylvestro figured we would not be required at Le Stage that evening. However, he'd prearranged a gig or two for us in Toronto for a couple of days, on a stretch of Yonge Street known as Yonge Street Strip. It had an extremely high concentration of old and new music venues all along the strip.

Many of the establishment specialized in providing music of a certain type or genre, and so there was something for everybody; not just crooning eh!

It always gave Severine and me a chuckle because although Toronto clubs were prohibited from serving alcoholic drinks after 11pm, there was, however, a get-out subsection to the rule which outwitted it.

Severine had done the strip before she and I became paired. She explained to me thus: "In the event that customers order food with their drinks, it's perfectly OK. Even if the so-called 'food' is merely a saucer with celery sticks and carrots. Wine's in, wit's out eh!"

It oftentimes is the case that the established law per se cannot handle a situation of perplexity that requires even a speck of brain power. The same may be said regarding the Mafia law as such.

Our boss Sylvestro 'Silver Dollar Sam' Carollo is an unmitigated law unto himself. However, of late, we have heard that the Rizzuto crime family (based in Montreal) is recognized as an independent family – often referred to as the "sixth family". With regard to laws and 'family' values, hopefully never the twain shall meet!

Our grandpa was right when he declared to us kids: "If your foresight was as good as your hindsight, you'd be too quick-witted and smart by a damn sight!"

22

Corresponding

I can say:
nothing deeper
more simply
or greater.
Here:
before your feet
I scatter
full of longing
the rich-petalled blossom
of my life

Those twins who played the terrifying sisters in Stanley Kubrick's definitive classic *The Shining* have done what we did, they have both grown up. I read somewhere that today the 'spirited' sisters live somewhat discretely in the UK. Lisa is still active as a lawyer and Louise as a published scientist.

It was as children too that Severine and I almost became household names. After Mom died, our garish guardian Aunt Helena put our names forward for a TV commercial competition. We did OK and made several public appearances which eventually transitioned us into the arms of a theatrical syndicate.

We came to be advertised and billed as: *Dynamantic Twins*, *Talented Siblings* and, more recently, as *The Kowarsky Twins*. However, after our father's conspiracies became headlines, we simply became known as *Severine and Ricky*. It seemed that our reborn monickers had almost come to encapsulate the very essence of nightclub music to a certain generation of followers.

Although we had finally got our indelible name out there at last, the pay was awful and, oftentimes, we were virtually broke. However, the 'Mob' (as they became known) were always pretty much on hand to offer us work at one or another of their establishments – our father's name was good for something!

Severine became known as "Princess" to many of the performers; however, the maestro was altogether rude when he suggested that Severine and I were not merely on the periphery of the Cosa Nostra but more likely part of it![4]

---

4   In the Mario Puzo bestselling novel *The Godfather*, the author creates a character named Johnny Fontane, a singer who is 'owned' by the Mob. Press reports imply that, in a similar fashion, Severine and I are tarred with the same brush. This mistaken belief doesn't pertain to either of us.

23

Mike Bellisarious

Dreams can run into reality
and once or twice
the dream can work.
Especially in the end
when reality dissolves
completely into dream.

We'd come to a crossroads in our story where the choice of not mentioning Mike Bellisarious had been an issue to me. However, it should never have been an issue because 'Mike's story' is very much significant to our story and I would be short-changing the reader had Mike been left out.

It's crucial that all the unbiased facts and the dirty stuff should be included, clear and precise, and that nothing is left to the imagination, either yours or mine. In some respects, I think that RD would have gained more credibility and, indeed, been able to have influenced the reader to a greater extent by not mentioning the existence of our Mike. However, it's said that truth is stranger than fiction, so here's the truth, warts and all!

Speaking for myself, I'd never shot a person with a bona fide gun, although I did shoot one of my playmates with a slug gun when I was a kid. However, not so our Mike, he carried at least one .32 automatic at all times and two if he intended to use it. It was also somewhat unusual to find Mike without 'muscle' accompanying him – "just in case things got rough", he'd say. In some respects, he'd made a rod for his own back inasmuch his reputation preceded him and there were many antagonists who would be stupid enough to contretemps him.

Uncle Mike was ruthless particularly when his strong sense of moral values was tested. Folks asserted that his moods could modulate, it wasn't so much his moods as his old-fashioned modus operandi, that's what folks didn't grasp. Even young fast-climbing villains tended to avoid him, rather than hero worship him, for fear of his capricious ways. There are so many yarns about our Mike's behaviour, some just high jinks, some out and out atrocious. Here's one that gives me a chuckle every time I think of it:

On one occasion, at a club in New York, Joe Gallo, a Mafia Boss, had been dating this beautiful air hostess. That, in itself, was OK but unbeknown to her, he had been boasting about his exploits all over town. He had no way of knowing that the hostess was one of Mike's recurrent girlfriends. To cut a long story short, Joe was manhandled to a tenement basement in New Jersey, where Mike kept a caged lion who would become displeased when poked with a billiard cue. Apparently, Joe apologized profusely, on his knees at one stage; and that was that! One boozy evening Joe divulged his impartiality towards air hostesses and especially lions!

*

I guess what sums it all up for Severine and yours truly is just the other day when a member of the Sylvestro Carollo fraternity, realizing our family connection with Mike observed: "I don't believe in God, however I'm afraid of God, on the other hand I *do* believe in Mike Bellisarious and I'm afraid of him dead or alive" ... plain spoke or what?!

Peter Kowarsky was our absent parent. He finally went to prison serving a 14-year sentence for his part in extortion, illegal gambling and loan-sharking. Shortly after his sentence began, it's rumoured that Mike had him killed. The rationale behind it is a mystery, except that afterwards Mike disappeared.

As the years drift by, the great 'Mob' debate as to whether or not our Mike is still in the land of the living continues. Not one person wants to inadvertently run into this criminal masterclass on the off-chance that he doesn't want to be found!

Whether the tales of his terror years are beginning to become over-exaggerated – merely overplayed superstition, is too complex by far. Usually spoken be an unintelligent few with nothing to lose!

24

Toodle-pip Reg and Ron

I wish for you …
vintage wine
in every Coca-Cola glass
and an end to wishing —
— assuring me you've found
your forever,
now!

It's not often that the mailman has occasion to knock on our door with recorded delivery, however an impending visit from Reg and Ron Kray was the reason why. We were pleased that they contacted us and that we weren't just ships that passed in the night and, in any event, we felt that we owed them for their hospitality and ongoing helpfulness whilst we were in the UK.

Apparently, they'd initially had difficulty in obtaining a landing visa into the United States, pertaining to their criminal records. Reg explained that eventually they were put in touch with an American business man called Alan Cooper – an international Mr Fix-it, who arranged permission for Reg and Ron's stay in the United States for one week only.

Severine and yours truly were there to welcome them when they debarked at Kennedy. It all seemed rather surreal to us, inasmuch that several burly officers from the FBI were also there to meet them! I guess it was a fairly run-of-the-mill operation for them, but for us the atmosphere was super electric!

By all accounts the twins were in NY in order to chew over dealings with a person called Frank Ileano. He turned out to be head honcho of the New York Mafia. Whilst they all headed off to a prearranged meet at a house in Brooklyn, Severine and I prepared for our evening show at the Taft Hotel.

Around midnight the whole kit and caboodle of us rendezvoused in the Taft lounge for drinks and a light meal. It was all very congenial – I guess that everyone there had similar interests! We managed to get a few valued moments alone with Reg and Ron and, pretty soon after, we all retired to our bedrooms.

By the early morning, everyone had gone their separate ways. Indeed, that was the last time we saw Reg and Ron. As time went by, we heard, via the grapevine, that they had become guests of Her Majesty. Folks say "take as you find". In the short time we knew the Krays, Severine and yours truly considered them as friends!

25

Ruth Magdalene Minnelli

I will be for you
whatever works.
I will work for you
to make you 'b'.
while you eliminate for me
the buzzing in my brain and so —
— in case you didn't already know!

It seems to me that some of the most indicative signs of a woman being a whore are not as upfront as you would imagine. Capable of being easily influenced by feeling or emotions and finding acceptability among other fashionable young urban people are, to me, sure signs and a sure indicator of whorish behaviour.

It wasn't so much that our boss, Sylvestro 'Silver Dollar Sam' Carollo, needed now to be especially on his guard over his choice of his current broad; it's more along the lines that he should be more attentive toward her as a devalued person, which is what she is. She is unquestionably an intelligent and certainly adaptably talented young woman. For all of her sins, she can be larger than life – given the opportunity. Oftentimes, we invite her around to our apartment and her tales sure give us a titter or two. However, to be totally candid, it seems, at times, that it's only Severine and I that are rooting for her – Sylvestro's workforce refers to her as an "abomination". It's so sad; she has written down in her pocketbook some of the disdaining words they have used: "peppery, intractable", and she beamed from ear to ear "monomaniacal" … "I've not come across that expression before" she laughingly confessed.

Ruth continued to tell us about her joys and her sorrows: "You two love me, don't you?" and she gave us a huge smirk: "men like me because I look like a girl who could steal their husband – not for too long though" she laughed aloud!

Yes, our buddy and Sylvestro's whore: Ruth Magdalene Minnelli is, indeed, larger than life but what concerns me of late is that she is also a close friend of the Rizzuto family!

26

"Don't You Dare Ask God to Help Me"

Come to me in solitude
pushing through the crowd
there are no others here
To pry or make demands.
If no one waits for you
but me,
I wait in that same solitude
that brings you here.

"Did you see them remonstrating in Mont Royal Park today Ricky" Severine paused, waiting for Ricky's reply. "You mean Women's Lib – poor little things, their faces looked so bitter and twisted" he solemnly replied and continued: "I think they actually enjoy being peevish and bitter and kicking up all holy hell, what say you Severine?" ... "It's exactly the same with their male counterparts Ricky when they challenge the bourgeoisie – they imitate the so-called Marxist and Lenin views of their grandaddy and cause as much rumpus as the can when, in actual tough-minded terms, they are pussies!" Ricky added: "The little bit of damn good they all achieve is not even negligible eh!"

After their points of view had been aired, Severine and Ricky headed out to L'Habitant for lunch. The food there is expensive; however, the quantity is great value. They both generally skip the wine for a jug of ice-cold water instead, which compensates and counterbalances the overall cost.

*

The Kerstins

The Kerstin Sisters – Katherine and Mathilda – were in cabaret at L'Habitant that evening and, having heard so much about them, we wanted to catch their performance from the beginning.

The audience were enthusiastic and called for a couple of encores and so it was moderately late before the punters disappeared and the establishment closed. We asked the sisters if they would join us for drinks in the swanky after-hours bar, which they eagerly did; being doyennes of entertainment does have its advantages!

Although the sisters were relatively young – in their twenties – they were both so filled with confidence, ambition and the determination of professionals twice their age. Put me so much in mind of Severine and yours truly when we were their age – they had what many entertainers call "a spark of divine fire". The somewhat older Severine and Ricky have learned that it's also immensely crucial to enjoy yourself and still have fun as well!

27

Sex is Much Better with a Woman

If I could say
face to face to you
in rhyme
or out of reason
why I feel this way
this day.

After only one night's
reading of you,
if I could say it straight
without complexity,
so that you and everyone
can understand completely …

… then I would be able
to write my final poem
and be done!

Severine and I have gone through an extremely drawn-out apprenticeship together. We absolutely spent time enough being irritated nobodies and had made up our proud minds that when we finally eat the cake and the cherries, we will be every inch the stars that folks are expecting of us. When, eventually, all of our dreams came tightly together, our names outside of clubs and marquees was all the Mob needed to set the cash registers ringing. Perhaps indeed that was the overriding consideration that kept the diverse ruling families so amicable for so many years and the bond was made. It's somewhat ironic really that once the piper had been paid and the chips were down, we were entirely content to entertain, enjoy scrummy meals and be able to afford well-heeled clothes! However, I guess it was somewhat different with Katherine and Mathilda because they have all their lives before them, whereas we've knocked a few years up!

I really am undecided as to what would have happened to Katherine and Mathilda in the long term, had Severine and I not taken them into our charge. Or now, looking back, was it actually them that instigated the whole involvement? 'Infatuation' can be an unpredictable and yet capricious alliance at times, in fact an emotion that you would rather not have at all! However, how would you define it? It's a lot more than a 'crush' but is it less than 'love' itself? Perhaps infatuation is more to do with passion and pleasure, perhaps simply an obsession of yours and their mind and body?

For the purpose of this novel, asking for a deep-seated confirmation of something the author doesn't entirely understand is like endeavouring hard to tell in from out at a Mongolian cluster-fuck. To achieve an answerable response from me is out of all realms of sanity!

My only conclusion that can be some sort of resolve; by using logical thought and not mathematics; by being avant-garde rather than ignoring the truth; and finally to be 'snappy' and get on with life, is to accept the fact the Severine is fucking Katherine and Ricky Mathilda … period!

It seems, to yours truly, that the so-called 'relationship' between Severine and Katherine had to have been made in heaven, inasmuch that is doesn't matter to them whether you are male or female – they copulate with anyone whom they find attractive!

I've come to know
your body and eyes,
like a fairy tale
a child might memorize.

I require your reading
most every night,
like a child would
so don't lose sight …

… of even one dragon
or of a single tree,
all of them
belong to me.

And when I ride through you
like a zealous knight,
and all your soul
you do bequest.

Just as a child
I shall request,
you read the part
I like the best.

28

Masculine Mind *Versus* Dominating Personality, *Versus* Double-Entendre

I would take a guess that yours truly was around 12 or 13 years of age when he began dating in a fairly earnest and frivolous manner. My train of thought was unquestionably predisposed to having sex, even if it only amounted to a fondle and a quickie. I was also prone to falling in love and suffering when it went face downwards, as it invariably did.

During those dismal days of increasing my testosterone, I also developed something of a sixth sense to alert me that I was indeed falling in love with the chick! I didn't ever make much dough in my combined jobs as busboy and singer, but I always knew that I was seriously in love because I wanted to spend my last-chance 10 bucks on the girls! It's kind of bizarre how young teenagers adopt their very own set of iffy values toward girls and being in love.

My beloved younger brother Mike, when he was a teenager, was the jazziest guy in the whole box of crayons. However, when he was a youngster I do believe he lacked a heart, inasmuch that his methodology for dating was: *"find 'em, fool 'em, fuck 'em and forget 'em!"*

Invariably there is a never changing factor with being a part of the complex gentle sex. You are solemnly deemed to be acquiescent, submissive, intelligent and charming with a sense of humour too! You would image that some of these qualities ought to also apply to the male of the species; however, yours truly would speculate it's rare: a man is a man is a man! Infuriating it oftentimes must be to negotiate the present day into yesterday's landscape, with a gentle sex body and together with a brain.

All of the gobbledegook regarding sex censorship and such is done and dusted, inasmuch that I want to deliberate upon the genuinely drop-dead gorgeous Mathilda Kirstin and her connoisseur of beauty, me – Ricky.

They had just luxuriated in the music of the McGill Chamber Orchestra – one of Montreal's best – at Place des Arts. In the carriage ride to Bonaventure Hilton they both are still in awe and admiration of the performance; libidinous libidos were playing a rhapsody or earnest too! Her hand felt delicate and elegant as he helped here step down from the carriage: "May I ask you a question Mathilda?" he enquired in a whisper: "Mathilda my darling, you have unscrambled me with such profound precision this evening. My somewhat sanguine question to you is, do you also acquit yourself to me?"

"Must be something to do with the totally relaxed atmosphere of that restaurant, because it seemed to me that I just talked, talked and talked, and you, my darling, just kept talking right back! When I heaped you with romantic words, you again kept on coming back, heaping your words on me also."

They paused in the entrance to the hotel lobby – it was still and hushed that time of the evening. He leaned over and gently bit her naked shoulder – perhaps entering her blood forever. She responded and lightly bit his tongue. "You know that something is going to happen when we reach our suite" he warned. What d'ya say Mathilda, *Double-Entendre* or what?"

Now, talk was senseless, her eyes said it all. Surprisingly soon, both were locked together by tongue and shoulder – past the teeth, past the lips – it was purely just a matter of who would take who down! That fatal barrier between soul and soul, and soul and self, was positively kaput until hell freezes over!

29

She Did It the Hard Way

I know I am desperate
when in your arms
and more so
when you're away.

I wind my watch
when it doesn't need winding,
I puzzle puzzles
more than my mind comprehends.

By these simple anecdotes
I ward off facing,
yet another confrontation
with your absence.

On the far side of town, Severine and her Katherine were both impeccably dressed in elegant shimmering gowns. Shepherded by the restaurant usher, they made their way across the Ritz-Carlton cocktail lounge to table number 66. The seats shuffled, as though choreographed, for them to be seated, Prior to taking her seat Katherine leaned forward – with the predatory grace of a Brando or Nicholson – and kissed Severine full on the mouth! "Curious how a snog is au fait with the whole restaurant – all up to speed eh!" Severine liked her little one-liners. "I enjoyed my snog dear Katherine, perhaps at heart I am a man!" Severine popped a question across the table to Katherine: "Kath, why do you take as many lovers?" She replied smiling: "They asked!" She continued: "I think it's because I adore being home at last in Canada, in the United States sex is just an ill-considered suggestion, whereas in Canada it's an obsession! Women in the States don't fully understand their sexuality. For example, my legs are my most eminent asset – I know just what to do with them too!"

I learned that most women Kath courted may have been somewhat less famous than the men she courted but, nevertheless, they seemed to be no less numerous. What I do adore about my Severine is the way she has with words that always tend to give me a chuckle. I oftentimes wait up for her when I know she's out on a so-called blind date – with female or male, both can be sometimes dubious!

When she finally comes home to roost, I'm usually propped up on a pillow watching an old Cagney movie – they oftentimes show those 1930's movies late at night. I was nearly asleep when she came home on Saturday night but managed to ask: "How'd it go?" Her answers were always pretty much alike: "I gave him a sexual and moral cleansing – both" she replied. In the event her date had been a woman, Severine's customary reply was more deferential in nature: "Sucked every last drop of resistance out of her". Always said so nonchalantly too!

30

Unfamiliar Evenings, Distant Music

Thank you for the sun you brought this morning, even though the sky was full of clouds. And thank you for holding me in your dreams, and steering me through those noisy crowds.

Now as you lie sleeping,
sparingly I'll take a break,
to tell you things I never say
when you are wide awake

They had their own unique individuality, almost too unique for the times we live in. During and after courting our Katherine and Mathilda that awesome summer, Severine and I also began to capture some of their uniqueness.

The four of us were working five or six evenings per week at separate venues, however after the curtain went down, we would scurry off to our separate lovers. Once a week we'd make up a foursome but, by and large, our evenings were spent in a state of undress. Notwithstanding the lateness of the hour, we all seemed to be in better health for it!

Speaking for Severine and Ricky this was indubitably the first occasion in their joint professional lives that sex, romance and passion had found its way into their workaholic lives. Why? This type of impetuously quintessential tug on the heart strings can only be felt; never analysed.

Says Ricky: "I shall always recall the moments when Severine and yours truly returned to our apartment in the early hours of the following day, completely washed out. After our respective nightclub cabarets, the four of us decided to go bebopping at the Rue Ste Catherine Est Metropolis and it was just the straw that broke the camel's back! Our partners had duly returned to their own apartment whilst Severine and I just threw our tired bodies onto our Chesterfield and lay for an eternity in each other's arms. Sounds silly, but we were just so elated by the joy our new lives had seemingly bestowed upon us, we cried and cried prolifically!"

Says Severine: "Ricky dear brother, you do realise don't you that you and I are not really worthy or rightfully due to be given this type of profound happiness – and a successful cabaret show to boot!" Severine gave me one of her cheeky smiles: "Just to underscore our good luck Ricky, you do realise don't you, that when all this sparkling effervescence is done, we are both going straight to hell!" They both quietly chuckled until Ricky imprudently asked: "Ever done this much 'posturing' previously little sis?" Severine stared fixedly at him for a moment or two, and then replied: "I am always 'posturing' of late Ricky, how about you – how do *you* get by?" Ricky answered in a matter of fact way: "Speculatively speaking, I'm practising and getting rather skilful at it!" He then responded: "Together we will conquer the world sis". Severine, thoughtfully reflective, added: "Our audiences always sound as though they're glad to see us, and I'm damned glad to see them too – what say you, Ricky?"

31

Sex or Love?

I never sleep half so well
as when I'm sleeping next to you
nor talk quite half as much
as when I talk direct to you.

My hand whilst reaching for your face
is reaching for the Moon or Mars.
As sure as God has shown me
I am reaching for the stars.

Severine's snoozing – Ricky's talking!

"When I was younger, I had an unfortunate habit of not being able to have a sexual liaison with a woman, without falling hopelessly in love with her. How absolutely crazy is that, because all illusions so often die. However, and speaking as a singer of love songs, I guess there's some kind of mystique and musical purity about it. Now that I am older, I believe that nothing can take the place of real true love … or can it?"

*

"In any event, it's natural for the young to go banging about, and falling in love so willy-nilly is just power for the course eh!"

*

"However, I like to kid myself that as I've grown more mature, that perhaps I have become a little more sensitive and it's not 'slam bang, thank you ma'am' anymore!"

*

"The problematic setback with yours truly is that he has made so many fucking mistakes in his relationships that, oftentimes, he awakes all hot and cold in the night, just being contemplative of all the fuck-ups he has been proficient enough to accomplish!"

*

"As I've grown more mature, I have indeed grown out of favour with simple lust. It seems to me that all women have a certain elegance and mystique about them which is somewhat destroyed when they strip down to their bare flesh. Mind you, in the event that you both have the hots, then total abandonment is by far better than restraint in the long run; isn't it?"

*

"Whilst we are on the subject of sexual scores; don't you agree that *kissing* is the most spectacular stratagem designed specifically by nature itself, to prevent speech when words become superfluous. Me, I'm all in favour of that form of communicative silence … what say you, Severine?"

*

Author's comment:

Love or indeed lust, it's fire unleashed; but oftentimes it's difficult to ascertain as to whether it's going to warm your hearth or simply burn your house down! However, with regard to losing your house, the sensible thing to remember is it's far more advantageous to have been unfaithful than faithful without wanting to be so … be warned!

32

Au Revoir #1

Some heroes
leave behind
a line to live by.
This one mentioned:
"if love were all".

Whilst Severine and yours truly were entertaining at Reg and Ron's, we were introduced to two second-to-none folk, Diana and Alan and, by and by, we became close buddies of theirs. We weren't to know at the time, but Diana was a phenomenal actress and entertainer herself. Diana Dors and her adoring husband and manager was Alan Lake.

As you have no doubt read in a previous chapter, Severine and I rather abruptly pulled out of the UK and returned to Montreal. Unfortunately, our ad hoc disappearance meant that Diana and Alan lost trace of us; however, they eventually located our whereabouts by approaching several Montreal agencies.

Apparently, Diana had agreed to do a comedy sketch at the Liverpool Empire; however, during the interim, Alan had been taken ill and, therefore, she was unable to fulfil her contractual obligation to them. She had mentioned us to them and they were willing to substitute, subject to terms etc. The remuneration was actually excellent. Diana said that class acts from across the pond were always well sought after.

Inadvertently, we would be needful of Katherine and Mathilda to temporarily cover our absence at Le Stage and for Sylvestro to agree as well. All I can add is that everything harmonized according to plan, even to Kat and Math booking a couple of days' vacation from their venues as well.

I wanted to add this remark that dear Diana made when I told her that everything was cool and as scheduled!

"I have been very happy, very rich, very beautiful, much adulated, very famous and, at times, very unhappy too. However, to be blessed with exemplary friends is indeed a gift from God!"

Finally, all of the arrangements transpired with Katherine and Mathilda happily relocating to our apartment whilst we were just temporarily chirruping away at the Liverpool Empire.

Three days into out UK visit, which was the second day of our agreed gig at the Empire, the hotel commissionaire handed us a surprise cablegram from Ruth Magdalene Minnelli in Montreal (you may recall, she is the young lady who prefers not to wear a brassiere!). Telephone tariffs being stiff in the UK, we scheduled a person-to-person call to Ruth that afternoon (morning, Montreal time) and wished to God we hadn't!

33

Au Revoir #2

We come into the world alone
we go away the same.
We're meant to spend the
interval in closeness.
However, it's a long way
between the morning and the evening.

Ruth's opening gambit told us in no uncertain language: "Don't the pair of you ever return to fuckin' Montreal!" She had kind of laid herself bare by contacting us and right now she was rattling on at a rate of knots. So much so that Severine and I were somewhat losing track of what Ruth (though succinctly trying) was striving to put across to us! However, we precisely got the gist of her warning and unequivocally thanked God that we were in England!

Our friends and lovers, Mathilda and Katherine, had been murderously slain whilst they slept – premeditation, by a contract killer!

Ruth continued to screech down the telephone: "Don't you grasp what's gone down, isn't it plainly obvious? The hit guy wrongly assumed that you two kids were asleep in that bed!" I managed to get a word in edgeways to dear Ruth in order to break into the somewhat lively conversation: "Unthinkable though it is, due to the girls being mistakenly murdered, the contract, as such, is still approved and upheld – regardless!" The transatlantic call time terminated and that was indeed the last time we heard from our Montreal buddy Ruth.

Ricky and Severine never performed in public again, nor indeed ever let it unintentionally slip that, as a twin duo, they had earned unqualified admiration during a career which, to date, spanned nearly 30 years.

An unconfirmed rumour on the street says that eventually they retired to Paris, France. Ricky writes novels and Severine offers piano coaching at neighbourhood schools. They are both happy and, although Paris is 'cool', it doesn't belong to them in the way that 'their' Montreal did!

Addendum

Banditry, the protection racket, bribery, secret justice societies and, last but not least by any stretch, are the families themselves. These are but a few of the more distinct and significant components that created the Mafia per se and are still in existence today. More effective than courts and tribunals, it's a system before whom members are under oath sworn to obey its judgements.

Although Severine and Ricky were never in truth actually sworn into the system they had indeed gone along with it by assigning their interests to a 'family' of influence. This move, in effect, put the onus of responsibility for Severine and Ricky's wrongdoings – no matter how naïve or gullible – into the 'family's' hands. When push came to shove, it was indeed Severine and Ricky's guilelessness that sentenced them. Inasmuch that their personal 'guardian' had been put under such strong pressure to satisfy the system and had little or no alternative but to sanction their execution – to save and retain an equilibrium of sorts. To cut a long story short their execution would be in the best interests of all those concerned.

In the present circumstances Severine and Ricky have been fortunate in finding a 'hiding place' and an interminable search for them could be costly and never-ending. Seems to me that unless told otherwise, totalitarianism may have, on this occasion, lost the toss!

It's been suggested to me that what is bizarre and somewhat incomprehensible is that the word 'Mafia' derives from the Arabic *mafia* or *place of refuge*! Whatever the word's origins, I do hope and trust that all the folks identified with that notorious and fabled word will just subsequently involve themselves in more pressing operations!

The Sequel: The After-Effect

There can be many pivotal points in a person's life when they slip and fall down Alice's rabbit hole and unexpectedly find themselves subliminally and significantly changed. Right there and then, they began to see themselves as totally a different entity than they had been previously. They can oftentimes see themselves in entirely different time frames and in places and situations other than the ones they have been accustomed to.

For a number of years Severine and yours truly relocated somewhat, here, there and everywhere. In some respects, we kind of dreaded each new location, wondering in trepidation if, in fact, it may be our last. And yet every passing minute we treated with open and natural smiles and buoyancy. It was true that we thought more about our physical comfort and lifestyle than we did about our safety and security – "choose wisely", I could guess at what our Mom would say.

We hunkered down in Oslo for several months; it was dissimilar to anything we knew before, but nice nevertheless. All of those tall Norwegians with seemingly beautiful clear skin, horns on their heads and cowbells ringing wherever you go! Finland we liked a lot too: clean, quiet and orderly and … fucking cold!

And 'mother' Russia where we spent two years, six months and three days! We tried despairingly to further our education by chewing the fat regarding art, music and architecture, to no avail! Most likely because our attention was often sidelined by potholes, large icicles hanging dangerously from above and pick-pockets on all sides! We did enjoy our strolls though, especially through Red Square and Gorky Park. Strange how we always had this underlying sort of subconscious feeling that somehow, we were trespassing!

It was just approaching the Christmas holiday season when we unintelligibly mellowed and had a strong inclination to spend our Christmas in Canada. Time-honoured tradition puts our Canada top of the list at Christmas – hell, the country is more than pragmatically made for Christmas!

We found ourselves a somewhat worse for wear, lonely old house, abutting an abandoned churchyard – we straight away christened the miscarry "Ghost Farm". The realtor wasn't certain of the property status of the house, i.e. rental or buy? Said he'd sort it out after the holiday. Indeed, it was refreshingly pleasant to be back in our homeland – where being trustful is commonplace. Before Christmas began proper, Severine and yours truly really wholeheartedly sweated blood to make our little piece of heaven as Yuletide in every respect.

In harmony with our wild front garden is the heavenly Bethlehem Nativity, complete with stable. As you approach our front porch, we fixed a large plastic praying angel, which lights up. Two large elms in the back garden were perfect for strings of lights hanging from their agley branches. I've always been somewhat circumspect toward heights and so my dear sis Severine took over the chore of fixing fairy lights along the gutters and across the rooftop as well. Finally, together we installed a large red glowing Santa Claus and reindeer on the downward slope of the roof. Severine then began to decorate our seven-foot-tall tree, post haste, whilst yours truly fixed an illuminated large crucifixion scene upon our garage door. By the time I'd arrived in the foyer, I'd run short of tinsel and mistletoe, and so we just made do with a mimsy nativity scene!

Within just several hours of turning all of the Christmas lights on, it was like 'loaves and fishes'. It seemed to me that the entire village were scattering around en masse and arriving at speed to get a good peak at our resourceful caper. Foolhardy perhaps, because like a snake biting its own tail, we had put ourselves well and truly in the public eye – for better, or hopefully not for worse.

That evening our 'highway 20 attraction' made news on CHML and other local radio stations – alongside a pregnant woman who hitched a ride to the hospital on a snowplough – to bare her 'blizzard child'!

I think we both had a false sense of security out here in the sticks. Rationally speaking, who would have a poisonous intent to kill us in any event. There is an intimacy about this needful time-worn home of ours, and bad folks are not invited – "Go to hell, you bastards!" – I felt arrogantly overconfident!

That evening, after supper, we journeyed across to Scarborough, Ontario, to enjoy a gig put on by the Ramblin' Lou family singers: Lou Lou (Sr) on banjo and Joni Mitchell Lou provided vocals and ukulele. I had never encountered a zither before – one usually doesn't – however, that evening Linda Lou played one. It had a deep fretted keyboard and the players right-hand plucks with the fingers and also a thumb plectrum. It may sound simple, but I assure you it isn't!

We absolutely convinced ourselves that no hood is likely to stop us breathing, just because we've deviated slightly from our higgledy hidey-hole course for one single evening. Although Scarborough is indeed an eastern part of Toronto, we both felt that it would be extremely unlikely to attract an esteemed Camorrista. They typically hang loose at one of the more exclusive downtown establishments, indubitably, not the Apothecary Music Bar at 'Scarberia'. (Even the legendary Scarborough Bluffs are of late referred to as "Scarberia" Bluffs!)

Two of us on the lam and not an executioner in site. We relaxed at the bar during the performers' interval and congratulated ourselves on our one-upmanship – it had taken some resourcefulness though!

Great luminary Humphrey Bogart was oftentimes playing moody and sullen parts. Unquestionably, his natural range wasn't falsetto by any means. However, the piercing squawk that reverberated across the boozer – and that we knew of old – without doubt was! *"Of all the gin joints in all the towns in all the world, Severine and Ricky you have to walk into mine."*

To be continued

Also by Ricky Dale

Limberlost
A semi-biographical account of famous soprano Krystyna Comanescu, a virtuoso who has fallen from favour and seeks to bring her austere demons to rest.

Limberlost II The Legacy
This book is the captivating sequel to *Limberlost*; in which secrets galore are let slip and the truth is exquisitely unearthed.

Limberlost III The Prequel
The prequel to *Limberlost*, and a most profoundly in-depth telling of not only how it all began, but the why and the who as well.

Cloudburst
An extremely personal insight into the fact-based account of why lovers Dahlia Carriera and Sandra Comanescu choose murder as a way of life.

I Knew The Bride When She Used To Rock 'n' Roll
A charming and emotional spooky tale, based on true happenings, which has been described as "*Poltergeist* meets the *The Sixth Sense*".

The House On Dundas And Vine
A beautifully haunting story about very powerful love between ordinary people doing extraordinary things in a quite ordinary way. Essentially a true story.

Siobhan's Bitches
A menage a trois mini saga between infatuation and love
… another virtually true story from the pen of Ricky Dale.

Kiss Me Deadly
Canderlaria was like an Ontario summer. Ripe, hotly
passionate and oftentimes playfully capricious. She came
quickly and went as she pleased, although he was never
sure she would come at all or how long she would stay.

About the Author

Ricky Dale is a former singer and lyric writer. Although recognised as a gifted wordsmith in his adopted Canada, when he finally returned to the UK, he was virtually unknown. His revival received a kickstart after he diversified by writing novels – this is his ninth. Ricky lives in a rambling maisonette on the coast, near the picturesque town of Torquay.

https://rickydaleauthor.wordpress.com